1, 2, 3 TEAM!

By Susie Gardner

Mercer University Press
Macon, Georgia

MUP/ H924

© 2016 by Mercer University Press
Published by Mercer University Press
1501 Mercer University Drive
Macon, Georgia 31207

9 8 7 6 5 4 3 2 1

Books published by Mercer University Press are printed on acid-free paper
that meets the requirements of the American National Standard for Information Sciences—
Permanence of Paper for Printed Library Materials.

Book design by Burt&Burt

ISBN 978-0-88146-590-7

Cataloging-in-Publication Data is available from the Library of Congress

Manufactured by Thomson-Shore, Dexter, MI (USA); RMA112DR266, June, 2016

Since I can remember, I have been passionate about children's books. Even as a college basketball coach, I have read books aloud to my players. Each person has their own learning style, and my challenge is to use creative techniques in order to reach every player. Some of the most poignant stories are those meant for children, yet sometimes they reach adults on an even deeper level.

Each season brings a different theme to my program and one year our motto was Team Before Me or "TB4M." This is the motivation for my book. I want to teach children at a young age the importance of being part of a team.

1, 2, 3 Team! *is a dream come true for me. It is my hope that this book touches young lives and sets a foundation and desire for them to become part of a TEAM.*

TB4M

It was the first day of practice. Everyone, especially Zoey, was super excited.

And then it happened. The new coach walked into the gym.

"Hello everyone. If we are going to defend our championship we have a lot of work to do. We have a game in two weeks, so let's get started."

Zoey picked up a
ball and started
to shoot.

"Wait a minute," said Coach. "We are going to begin and end all practices and games with a huddle."

"What's a huddle?"
thought Zoey.

Coach gathered the team in a tight circle.

"Okay," said Coach. "Put one arm in the air and raise your hand up to the sky."

"When I say 'TEAM on three, 1-2-3,' yell 'TEAM' with all of your might!"

So at the very first practice, the players got in a huddle and Coach said, "TEAM on three, 1-2-3."

Everyone said "TEAM!" with great enthusiasm.

Everyone... but Zoey. Instead of "TEAM!" Zoey said, "ME!"

After all, team... me... "What's the big deal?" thought Zoey. I'm a very important part of the team. In fact, without me, we wouldn't win nearly as much as we do!

For an entire week, the Coach
would huddle the players and
say "TEAM on three, 1-2-3!"

At first, Coach didn't notice that someone was saying "ME" instead of "TEAM" because the two words sound so much alike.

But the next time the team was in a huddle, Coach made a point to see just who was saying "ME!"

Coach realized it was Zoey but did not let her know.

At the next game, Coach sent Zoey onto the court for the jump ball. But the rest of the team stayed on the bench.

"Where is everyone?" asked Zoey.

"All you need is 'ME,'
said Coach, "so go out
there and play against
the other team."

"But who will pass
the ball to me?"

"And how will I guard all five players?"

Finally, Zoey realized she needed her teammates. "I can't play with just me. I need the team."

After a few minutes, Coach gathered the team in a huddle. They all raised one arm in the air with their hand to the sky.

Coach said, "Okay, everyone. 'TEAM on three, 1-2-3' and EVERYONE yelled...

TEAM!

From that day on Zoey understood...

that no matter
how good she was,

she couldn't
play without
her teammates.

Before the next game, Zoey asked Coach if she could say something to the team.

So she got her teammates in a huddle
and everyone raised their hand to the sky.

Zoey yelled
"TEAM on
three, 1-2-3!"

TEAM!

TEAM!

TEAM!